For Kees & Hans
Nancy Kaufmann

For Fenna
Jung-Hee Spetter

Text copyright © 2003 by Nancy Kaufmann
Illustration copyright © 2003 by Jung-Hee Spetter
Originally published by
Lemniscaat b.v. Rotterdam under the title *Dag!*
Printed and bound in Belgium
All rights reserved
CIP data is available
First U.S. edition

Bye, Bye!

Nancy Kaufmann

PICTURES BY
Jung-Hee Spetter

Is it time for
school *already*, Daddy?
You come too.

We can play.

Don't go away!

I want you to stay

and read me a story

and make me fly!

Let's rub noses!

Oh, no! Teacher says you *really* have to go, Daddy!

Hey...

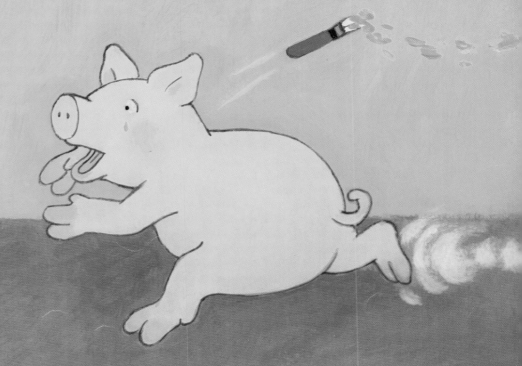

can I play?

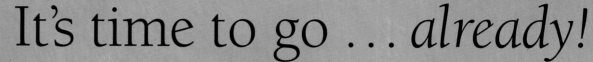

It's time to go ... *already!*

Bye, bye!